Dinosaur

Train

To Jesse, whose love of dinosaurs and trains inspired this story;

to Molly, for keeping all of our hearts buoyant;

and to Kathie, for sharing (and enduring) this dream with me.

Dinosaur Train

Copyright © 2002 by John Steven Gurney

Manufactured in China. All rights reserved.

For information address HarperCollins Children's
Books, a division of HarperCollins Publishers,
10 East 53 rd Street, New York, NY 10022.
www.harperchildrens.com

Library of Congress Cataloging-in-Publication Data is available.
ISBN 0-06-029245-8 — ISBN 0-06-029246-6 (lib. bdg.)

Typography by Jeanne L. Hogle
09 10 11 12 13 SCP 10
❖
First Edition

Dinosaur Train

story and pictures by

JOHN STEVEN GURNEY

HarperCollins*Publishers*

Thursday was a day much like any other for Jesse.

Trains and dinosaurs.

Dinosaurs and trains.

Just before bed, Jesse drew one last picture.

Suddenly there was a loud noise

and the whole house began to shake!

"ALL ABOARD!" someone shouted.

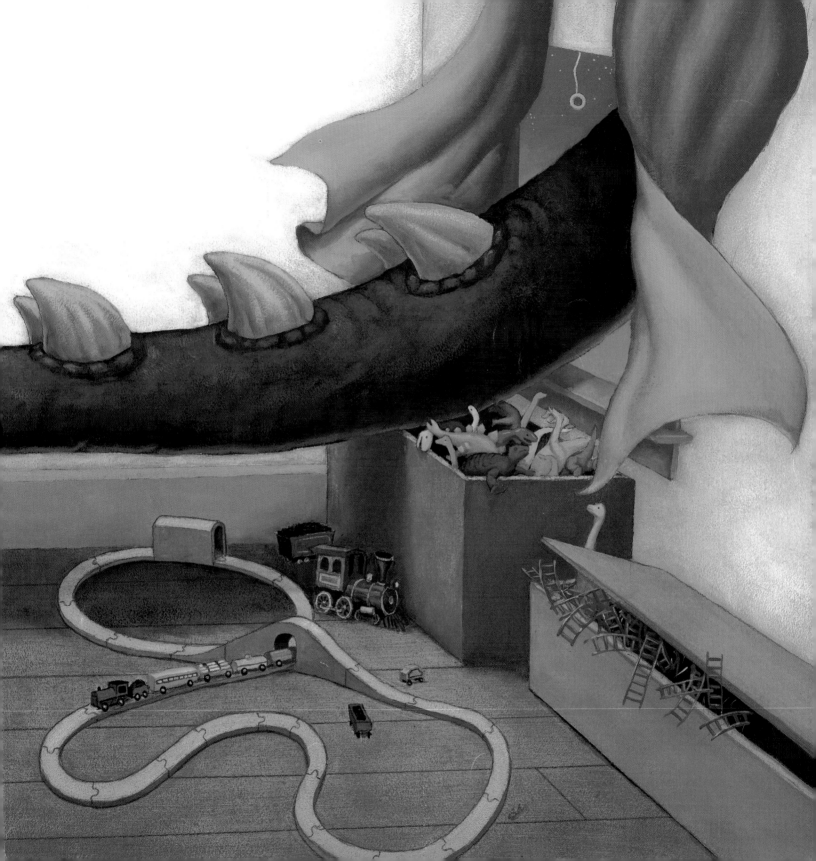

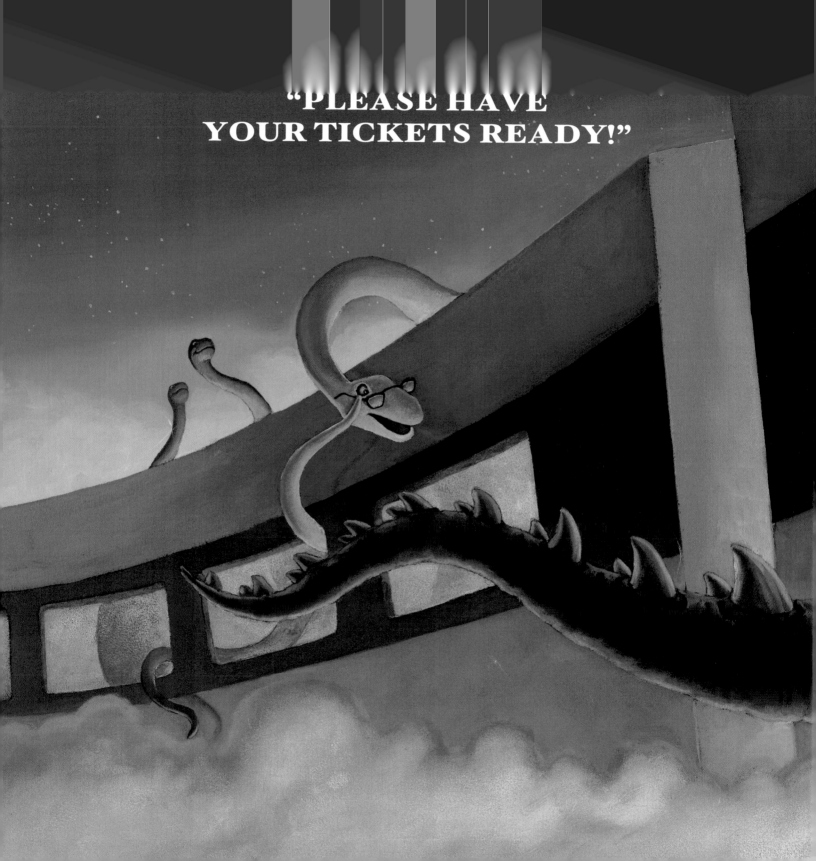

"Thank you," said the conductor.
"Dining car to the rear."

"Let me show you the view
from the sky windows."

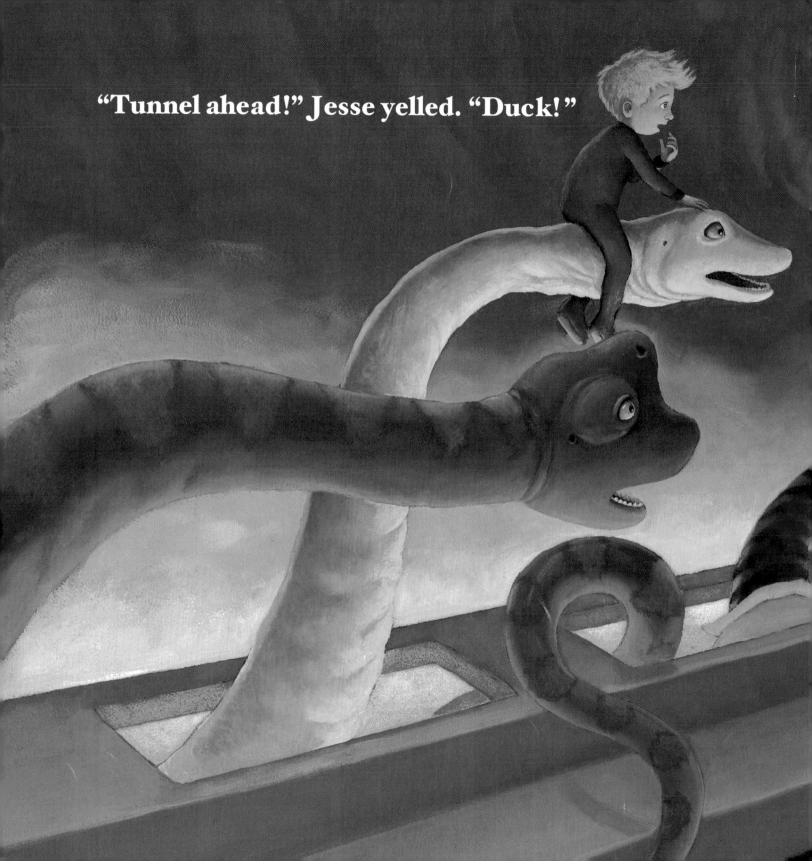

"Tunnel ahead!" Jesse yelled. "Duck!"

When they came out of the tunnel, Jesse said,
"Look! That's amazing."

Everyone leaned over to see.

UH-OH!

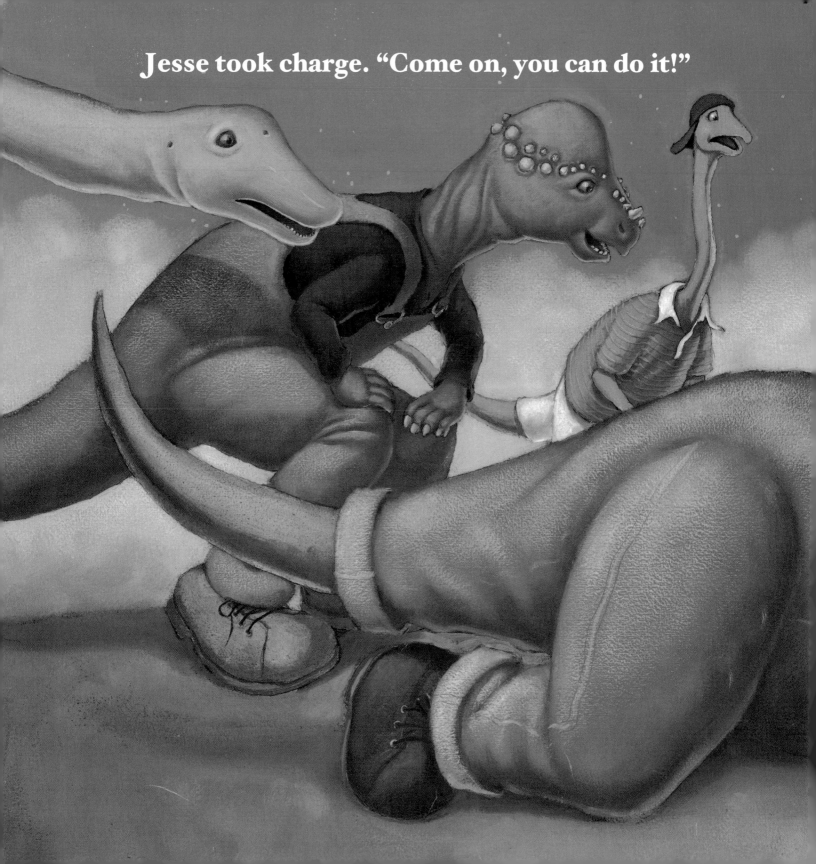

Jesse took charge. "Come on, you can do it!"

"Push it back on the track!"

"Thanks, son. You can ride up here with me."